For Max and Mason

First published in the United States of America in April 2013
by Walker Books for Young Readers, an imprint of Bloomsbury Publishing, Inc.
www.bloomsbury.com

For information about permission to reproduce selections from this book, write to
Permissions, Walker BFYR, 175 Fifth Avenue, New York, New York 10010

Library of Congress Cataloging-in-Publication Data
Yoon, Salina.
Penguin on vacation / by Salina Yoon. — First U.S. edition.
pages   cm
Summary: Penguin's tired of the snow and cold—so he decides to go on vacation!
But where should he go? And what new friends will he meet along the way?
ISBN 978-0-8027-3397-9 (hardcover) • ISBN 978-0-8027-3396-2 (reinforced)
[1. Penguins—Fiction. 2. Vacations—Fiction. 3. Beaches—Fiction. 4. Friendship—Fiction.] I. Title.
PZ7.Y817Pg 2013   [E]—dc23   2012032284

Art created digitally using Adobe Photoshop
Typeset in Maiandra
Book design by Nicole Gastonguay

Printed in China by C&C Offset Printing Co., Ltd., Shenzhen, Guangdong
1 3 5 7 9 10 8 6 4 2 (hardcover)
1 3 5 7 9 10 8 6 4 2 (reinforced)

Penguin on Vacation

Salina Yoon

WALKER BOOKS FOR YOUNG READERS
AN IMPRINT OF BLOOMSBURY
NEW YORK   LONDON   NEW DELHI   SYDNEY

"I need a vacation."
Penguin sighed.

Penguin had skied,

sledded,

and skated on vacations before.

He wanted to go someplace different.

Ninety-nine balls of snow on the ground...

Someplace . . .

"That's it! I'll go on
vacation to the beach!"
thought Penguin.

Penguin packed his bag
and headed north.

The waves swelled bigger and bigger.

The sun shone hotter and hotter.

Finally, Penguin reached the beach.

It wasn't what Penguin expected.

The beach
was nothing like
his icy home.

Penguin learned some things.

You can't ski on sand.

You can't sled on sand.

And you definitely can't skate on sand.

"Are you lost?" asked Crab.
"No, I'm on vacation,"
said Penguin.

"Then come with me!" said Crab.

Crab showed Penguin how
to have fun on the beach.

Sand castle.

Penguin and Crab played . . .

and played . . .

and played.

Penguin loved his new friend.

But all vacations come to an end.

It was time for Penguin to go home.

The journey was long and quiet,

but suddenly, something moved
in the water.

"Crab?! What are you doing here?"

"I need a vacation, too!" said Crab.

Penguin and Crab finally reached the shore.

They swam and swam.

They whooshed and pushed.

They fished and wished.

But all vacations come to an end.

Good-bye, Crab.

Crab set off for home and left behind . . .

. . . the sound of the beach.

"I shell return," wrote Crab.

So Penguin waited.

And one day, Crab did!